PIERINO and the BELL

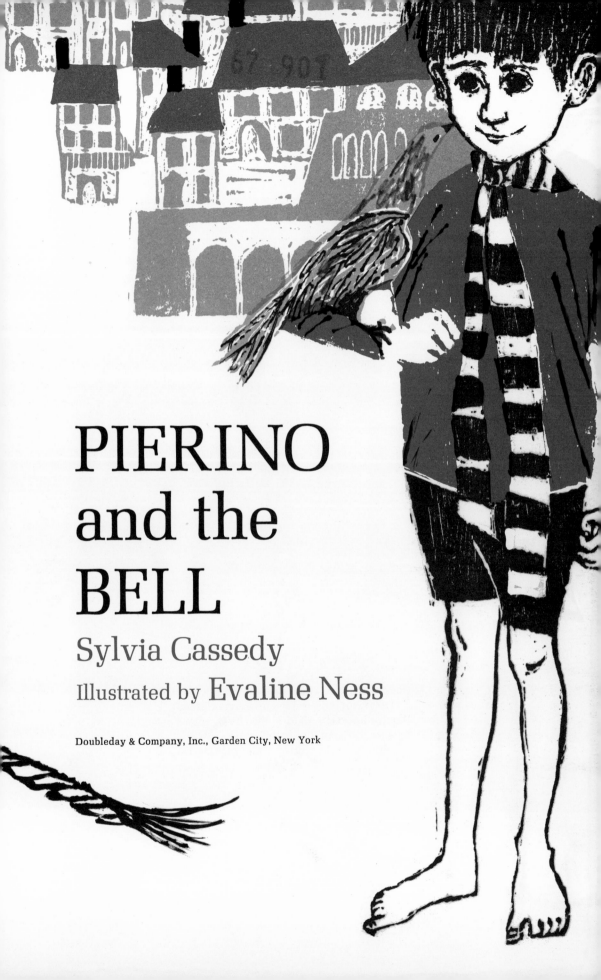

PIERINO
and the
BELL

Sylvia Cassedy

Illustrated by Evaline Ness

Doubleday & Company, Inc., Garden City, New York

For Ellen, Steven and Amy

Far away in the hills of Tuscany lay a very small village.

In the center of the village was a public square, and in the center of the public square stood a stone horse—a great stone horse with large, raised hoofs and an angry head. Streams of water poured from the horse's nostrils and mouth, and splashed into a circular pool below.

Riding the horse was a brave stone warrior wearing a stone helmet on his stone head, and carrying a stone sword in his stone hand.

No one remembered his name.

Clustered around the square were dozens of yellow stone houses with straight black chimneys that stood on the red-tiled rooftops like stiff hats and sent occasional feathers of smoke curling into the sky.

To one side of the square stood a yellow stone church with a single stained glass window, purple and green as a pigeon's throat, and a tall, thin tower above the window.

High in the tower hung a massive bronze bell.

Surrounding the village were the hills of Tuscany—low, craggy hills, brown in the daytime, red as pomegranates when the sun began to set, black and whispering with secrets at night. Clumps of black-green cypresses stood here and there like shawled women, and seldom stirred.

High upon a hill stood a castle with great wooden doors, blue and red armorial flags, and four crenelated towers baring their teeth to the sky.

A narrow bridge crossed the river that separated the village from the hills and the castle. A rail along either side of the bridge kept all but the very small and the very tall from toppling into the water.

But visitors to the little village, when there were any, took no notice of the brave stone warrior astride his horse, or the church with its tall tower and bronze bell, or the little yellow houses with their stiff black hats, or the castle with its battlements biting the sky with giant teeth, or the bridge with is narrow rails.

All villages in Tuscany had all these things.

But no other village had pigeons.

And this one did.

Filling the square of the little village, covering every inch of space, bumping into the great stone fountain, scraping against the walls of the tall-towered church, brushing along the clusters of yellow stone houses, catching their beaks in each other's wings, raising sudden clouds of soft yellow dust, and leaving everywhere, everywhere, a network of tiny four-pronged tracks—crowds and crowds of pigeons.

Ten thousand pigeons.

Pigeons black,

Pigeons brown,

Pigeons gray as the morning sky.

Pigeons sleeping,

Pigeons waking,

Pigeons walking,

Pigeons marching,

Pigeons fighting,

Pigeons kissing,

Pigeons burying brittle beaks into their purple-green throats, and filling the air with their cry...

Crr, crr, crr.

All the pigeons in Tuscany crowded into one square of one little village.

Everyone wondered why.

Some people said it was because the grain that was gathered from the surrounding hills was better than the grain anywhere else in the countryside.

Some said it was because the village was cooler than others.

Some said it was because the village was warmer.

But Pierino, the churchwarden's son, had heard from his father and his grandfather that the birds had come to the village all on a single day—the day, centuries before, when the mighty bronze bell had struck its first note. As the very first echo tumbled from the tower, the sky had suddenly grown stormy with the black of pigeon wings. Pigeons flew in from all over the countryside, and whirled around the square like leaves in a gale. They had come to listen to the bell, Pierino had been told, and they would leave only when the bell would ring no more.

No man or woman in the village believed Pierino's father or his grandfather or Pierino himself.

Only the children believed him.

"It *is* the bell that brings the pigeons," they would say. "Someday, Pierino, everyone will believe you. The pigeons themselves will tell."

"Yes," Pierino would answer. "The pigeons themselves will tell. They will tell me, and you, and everyone in the village. Someday," he would whisper, "perhaps," and he would return to the yellow stone church.

At noon each day and again at six, Pierino would leave his little room at the rear of the church, and climb the two hundred steps to the belfry high in the tower to pull the heavy bell rope. Twelve times at noon and six times in the evening, he would send the mighty clapper crashing against the great bronze dome of the bell. One after another, thunderous peals would roll over the square and out to the hills.

At this signal, like the lifting of a huge black sail in the wind, the ten thousand pigeons would rise from the ground and scatter to the heights of the village—to the helmet of the warrior astride the marble horse, to the straight black chimneys on the red-tiled roofs, to the black-green cypresses huddled on the hills, to the crenelated towers with their rows of giant teeth, to the flagpoles on the castle, to the railings on the bridge, to the yellow stone doorways, to the yellow stone sills—to the top of the tall bell tower itself.

High in his tower, Pierino would stand at his bell until the shadow of the last black wing had fluttered across his cheek, and all was still. Then he would lean from the little arched window and look at the pigeons dotting the village like speckles on an egg.

"They are listening," he would whisper. "They are listening to the echoes of the bell. How still they are!"

In the square below, the children would rush from their doorways, and play about the fountain, running, skipping, leaping, and erasing with their feet the four-pronged tracks in the soft yellow dust.

Then, when the final echoes of the bell had rolled across the sky like a thundercloud, and the village was still again, the pigeons would return one by one, floating down like leaves and filling the air with the cry in their throats...crr, crr, crr.

Once more the square would be black, and brown, and gray as the morning sky, and Pierino would descend the two hundred steps from the tower.

"Did you see how still the birds were?" he would ask the villagers. "Did you see? They were listening to the echoes of the bell."

"Listening?" the villagers would ask, surprised. "Listening to the echoes of the bell? They were flying from its noise, Pierino," and one or two might laugh.

"No," Pierino would insist. "They do listen. They love the bell. They came to the village to be close to the bell, and they shall never leave so long as it is rung each day."

18

But the villagers would already be turning away, not hearing. "It is the cold air," they would say.

"It is the warm air."

"It is the grain. The grain that is gathered from the hillside."

One day each year would be celebrated by the villagers and the pigeons together.

On San Colombino Day—the feast of San Colombino, patron saint of the village and of the church—Pierino would climb, as on all other days, the two hundred steps to the belfry, and toll the noontime bell. But on this day, when the pigeons would rise from the square and scatter like a starburst to the heights of the village, no child would come out to run and skip and leap around the fountain, erasing with his feet the four-pronged tracks in the soft, yellow dust.

Everyone remained indoors—waiting.

For on this day, when the pigeons fluttered down once more to the square, one by one, they left behind them... a thousand snowy white eggs.

Eggs on the chimney tops, eggs on the window sills, eggs on the helmet of the brave stone warrior, eggs among the cypresses huddled on the cragged hills, eggs on the teeth of the crenelated tower.

Even atop the great bell tower itself...a single snowy white egg.

One thousand eggs in all.

As soon as the last pigeon had floated down to the ground, and the square was once again black, and brown, and gray as the morning sky, all the children of the village poured out of their doorways, carrying baskets and shawls and aprons and hats. Up to the rooftops they scrambled, away to the cypresses, off to the castle with the crenelated tower, up to the helmet of the brave stone warrior, high along the window sills, over to the bridge rails, up, up, up, gathering eggs in their baskets and shawls and aprons and hats.

20

The egg atop the bell tower always belonged to Pierino.

After the twelfth pull of the mighty bell rope, he carefully stepped out on the narrow window ledge of the belfry, and, very slowly, standing on his toes, slid his hand up along the yellow stone tower until he could feel the glossy surface of an egg beneath his fingers. Then he lowered his arm, and slipped the egg into his pocket.

"Perhaps," he said every year, "the birds have left an egg finer than all the rest—an egg for me and the bell. I should show it to all the villagers, and they would know, at last, how the birds love the ringing of the bell."

Not until he was safe within the darkness of the belfry did he remove the egg and examine it. It was large and white and beautiful. "Surely," he always said, "there is no egg finer than this."

At six o'clock, when Pierino rang out the evening hour and all the pigeons cleared the square, the children quickly arranged their eggs in a giant circle around the horse fountain. The sun was very low in the sky by now, and touched each egg with the palest pink, turning the egg-ring into an enormous string of pink beads. The children clapped their hands, and tried to keep the pigeons, now dropping from the sky, out of the way.

After Pierino had added his egg to the ring, he looked at it for a long while. "It is, after all, no different from the rest," he sighed, scraping the soft, yellow dust with his toe and turning from the fountain.

A great egg feast followed. Wonderful egg dishes were prepared, and the villagers ate, and sang, and danced a special pigeon dance, beating their arms like wings and striking at their chests with their chins.

And all the time, the ten thousand pigeons bustled around and around, bumping their fat bodies against one another, and pecking at the feet of the dancing villagers, while above the singing and laughing could be heard the cry from their throats...crr, crr, crr.

At the end of the feast, each child chose one of the remaining eggs to take home and care for. For three weeks the children tended their eggs, keeping them warm, turning them, and waiting.

Then, one day there emerged from each egg a new little pigeon, rumpled and soft and wet as an olive leaf fresh with dew.

The children watched over their baby birds, smoothing their feathers, teaching them to fly, and feeding them bits of grain gathered on the hillside, until they were big and strong and eager to join the others in the square.

Then, each child carried his pigeon out to the square on one finger, and shook it free while the noon bell tolled.

"Perhaps it will alight on my window sill," each said, trying to follow its flight into the rising black cloud of wings.

One year, on the morning of San Colombino Day, Pierino woke with a start, and listened.

Everywhere, villagers were preparing for the festival. Out in the square, men were scrubbing the long stone slabs surrounding the horse fountain. In their kitchens women were taking down their heavy pots and pans, and polishing them for the egg feast in the evening. Up in the attics of the yellow stone houses, children were opening windows to place little clumps of straw on the sills. Straw for the eggs, Pierino thought.

But the pigeons in the square were hushed. "How quiet they are," said Pierino, straining to listen. "They are whispering. Their voices are like the wind in the cypresses. What is going to happen?"

At noon, he climbed the two hundred steps to the top of the bell tower, and pulled the bell rope twelve times. Outside, the ten thousand pigeons rose into the air like thunder. In a little while, all was silent. Pierino waited. Then, one by one, the pigeons tumbled from the sky, filling the square with their bustling, fat bodies, and stirring the air with the cry from their throats... crr, crr, crr.

All the doors and windows flew open, and the children began their search.

26

High in his tower, Pierino tiptoed to the arched window, and stepped out on the narrow ledge, his heart beating with excitement. Very cautiously, he reached his hand up, up, up to the very top of the tower, and closed his fingers around the treasure awaiting him.

Back in the shadow of the great bronze bell, Pierino sat down and removed the egg from his pocket. He held it in the palm of his hand, and gazed at it in wonder. It was of the purest silver, and it shone like the moon. Pierino stroked it with one finger. It was as smooth as the polished dome of the great bronze bell. He rolled it against his cheek. It was as cold as the water splashing in the circular pool. He closed his eyes, and then opened them to look again.

"A silver egg," he whispered. "For me. For me and the bell. A silver egg from the birds."

When the sun began dropping low in the sky, coloring the hills red as pomegranates, and splashing the bell with a single fiery stripe, the children started back for the square, and Pierino rushed down the two hundred steps of the tower, cupping both hands around his precious egg.

Then, while all the villagers stood by, he added to the pale pink necklace around the horse fountain...a glittering silver clasp.

Everybody gasped at the sight of Pierino's egg.

"A silver egg!" the men and women cried. "A silver egg for Pierino!"

"A silver egg!" the children shouted. "A silver egg for Pierino. For Pierino and the bell!"

"For Pierino and the bell!" the villagers repeated.

"Hurrah for Pierino!" they cried all at once, and they marched him around the square on their shoulders.

"Hurrah for the bell!" shouted Pierino, waving his hands high in the air.

"Hurrah for Pierino and the bell!" the children shouted, and they danced and sang and laughed as they never had before.

When the festival was over, Pierino carried the silver egg carefully up the two hundred steps to the dark of the belfry, and laid it on a bed of straw.

For three weeks he kept watch over his egg, turning it each day, warming it with his hands, whispering to it, and wondering.

Then, one day, he heard from within the silver egg a tiny rattle, soft and muffled as a silver bell inside a tightened hand.

He knelt over the bed of straw and listened again, wondering.

All at once, the silver shell shattered like glass, and there emerged before Pierino's eyes a beautiful silver pigeon.

Pierino caught his breath. "It's like a star," he whispered, and he knelt beside the tiny pigeon as it spread its silver tail like a fan, and scratched the wooden floor with its silver claws. "A star with wings," he said softly, and he ran to the window to give the village the news.

From the square below, the children saw Pierino waving and flapping from the belfry like a startled bird, and they crowded to the church, wondering what had happened.

Soon, everyone had heard of Pierino's beautiful pigeon,
and the men and women danced and clapped their hands
in the square, while the children followed one another up
the two hundred steps to the belfry, and huddled over the
tiny silver bird.

"A silver pigeon," they whispered. "For Pierino and the
bell," and they reached out their hands to stroke its gleam-
ing tail, longing for silver pigeons of their own.

Pierino fashioned a large cage of braided straw and placed the silver pigeon inside. Day after day he cared for his bird, feeding it, warming it in the sun, smoothing its silver feathers, and singing to it as it slept: "Pigeon, pigeon, silver pigeon..."

But he did not let it out of its cage. "It belongs to me alone," he would say. "To me and the bell."

All the children of the village would come in twos and threes to visit the silver bird in its braided cage, bringing it grain from the hillside, bowls of water from the fountain, and fresh straw for its bed.

"When will you let it out, Pierino?" they would ask. "When will it fly?"

"I don't know," Pierino would answer, looking away, and he would reach his hand through the bars and carry the pigeon about on one finger.

And all the time the silver pigeon grew strong and sure-footed and more beautiful than ever before.

Each day at noon and again at six, at the ringing of the mighty bell, it would spread its wings against the cage, like a silver kite in the tangle of a tree, and grasp the braided bars with its silver claws.

"Stay, stay," Pierino would say softly. "Stay with me and the bell," and he would gently return the pigeon to the floor of its cage.

"When, Pierino?" the children continued to ask. "When will it fly?"

And one day he answered, "Perhaps not at all. Perhaps I shall keep it with me forever."

"Forever?" the children asked. "But the pigeon is big now, and strong. It must fly. It must join the other birds in the square."

"But it is my bird," Pierino answered. "It was given to me because I ring the bell. The pigeons meant me to keep it," and he offered the silver bird a row of grains from his finger.

The children looked at one another, and slowly descended the stairs. "It is Pierino's pigeon," they said sadly, "and not ours."

The silver pigeon grew and grew, until, with its wings outstretched, it nearly filled the little braided cage.

The children rarely came now. It was Pierino's bird, they said. Pierino, himself, gathered grain from the hillside and drew water from the fountain.

One day, when the pigeon was full grown, and the tips of its silver wings scraped against the braided bars of its cage, the children climbed the two hundred steps of the tower to speak to Pierino.

"See how large the pigeon is, Pierino," they said. "You must set it free."

Pierino shook his head. "It was a gift to me," he said. "A gift to me and the bell."

"Yes," said the children, "but the bell belongs to everyone. It is the village's bell."

Pierino looked at the children.

"The pigeons came to the village to listen to the bell," they continued, "long before you began to ring it."

Pierino was silent.

"The silver bird was a gift to us all," they went on. "To you and the bell and the village."

Pierino looked down at the straw on the floor.

"You are right," he said at last. "It is everyone's bell,"

and he ran his hand along its bronzed dome. "But there is only one bird. How can I give only one bird to an entire village?"

The children thought.

"We shall all see it in the square," said one.

"And so will you, Pierino," said another. "From the little arched window in the belfry you will see it gleam among the others like a silver pebble in a pond."

"And it will fly," said another. "Each day at noon and again at six it will fly with all the rest. Perhaps it will alight on my window sill."

"Or mine," said another.

"Or mine," said another.

"Or mine," they all said together.

"Or mine," said Pierino sadly, and he stroked the silver pigeon's long, silver tail. "Or mine."

"When?" the children persisted. "When will you give the silver pigeon to the village? When will you set it free, Pierino?"

Pierino thought. "On San Colombino Day," he answered at last. "Then I shall give the bird to the village. On San Colombino Day it will be free. Perhaps it will alight on all of your window sills. And on mine, too."

The children returned to the pigeon-black square, happy that the silver pigeon was to be set free at last, but thinking that Pierino was right—there was only one silver bird, and everyone would want it for his own.

Then, at last, it was San Colombino Day. The men of the village cleaned the stone slabs around the fountain, and the women polished their pots and pans, while the children stood inside, waiting.

Just before noon, Pierino knelt beside the braided cage and opened its little door. The silver pigeon hopped on his finger. Pierino carried it carefully to the window ledge, and sang:

> "Pigeon, pigeon, silver pigeon,
> Silver helmet on your head,
> Silver shield clasped to your breast,
> Begin your silver flight.
> Silver armor on your wings,
> Silver breastplate, silver sword,
> Fly, fly, fly, my winged knight!"

Pierino stretched his arm through the window. "I give you to the village!" he shouted. "For the Feast Day of San Colombino!" and he shook the bird free from his hand.

Down, down, down, the silver pigeon tumbled toward the square, until, with a tremendous beating of wings, it suddenly launched itself upward and rose steadily higher and higher in the sky.

Around and around it circled, now high, now low, "like a star come loose from the heavens," Pierino said, holding his breath as he followed its flight about the square.

The noon sun rose high above the village, and it was time to ring the bell, but Pierino did not turn. "Fly, fly, fly!" he shouted, trying to reach the tip of the pigeon's silver wing as it flashed by the tower. "Fly, fly, fly!"

Far out the window he leaned. "Where will it alight?" he wondered aloud. "On whose window sill will it rest at last? On mine? On mine? On mine?" And the great bronze bell hung silently behind him, its clapper as still as the sword of the stone horseman.

And then, a few at a time, the village's ten thousand pigeons suddenly began to follow the great bird's silver flight. Slowly at first, then faster and faster, they gathered

behind its silver tail and swept across the square, around the tower, down to the warrior, over the bridge, away to the hills, until, sailing like a silver boat, the beautiful pigeon suddenly shot into the heavens, spreading its huge black sail in the wind, up, up, up.

All the children, forgetting the bell, came out of their doorways at the sound of the rushing wings, and watched first in expectation and then in alarm as the silver bird, trailing its fluttering, flapping cloud of pigeons, soared higher and higher in the air; higher and higher, until all were out of sight, and the sky was bare.

For the first time in centuries, the noonday sun hung directly overhead and no rumbling echo rolled across the square. No pigeon tumbled from the sky.

The square shone yellow in the sun.

No wing fluttered.

No claw scratched.

No beak scraped at the yellow stone walls.

No cry came.

The children stood motionless as cypresses in the vacant square, longing for the lost pigeons, and squinting into the empty sky.

At last, they turned around and started for their doors, dragging their empty baskets and shawls and aprons and hats in the soft yellow dust.

High in the belfry, Pierino looked down at the silent yellow square, and up into the sky.

"What has happened?" he cried. "Where have the pigeons gone?" And then he remembered the bell.

"The bell!" he shouted, and he spun around to the heavy rope, and pulled it with all his strength.

"Come back! Come back!" he called with every pull.

"They will come now," he said, and he ran to the window.

The sky was as clear as a snowy white egg.

No pigeon came.

Pierino looked down at the silent yellow square, his fingers gripping the ledge.

"What have I done?" he cried. "Have they really gone? Will they never come back? Could they not wait, even a little while, for the bell to ring again?"

All at once he caught sight of something, and his eyes swept across the village, searching. Then he let out a joyous shout, and rushed to the bell. Over and over he swung the rope as he had never swung it before. One hundred times the bell crashed across the sky, while down in the village, startled children with their baskets and shawls and aprons and hats tumbled from their doorways and hurried like a flock of birds to the church, wondering what had happened.

Up the two hundred steps they raced, and down again.

Out on the square they spilled, tumbling and stumbling, while the ringing of their laughter and the rumbling of the bell mingled in a jumble of singing, crashing peals, and the yellow tower trembled in the sun.

Round and round the square they ran, waving their baskets and shawls and aprons and hats, and laughing louder and louder until the yellow stone houses shook, and far away on the hills the black-green cypresses quivered.

But Pierino laughed loudest of all.

For, all around the village, wherever he could see, lay a glitter of silver eggs—nestled in the helmet of the brave stone warrior, balanced on the surface of the stone horse hoofs, in and out the teeth of the crenelated tower, high among the chimneys on the red-tiled roofs, hiding in the corners of the yellow stone doorways, deep within the branches of the black-green trees, high upon the flagpoles of the wooden-doored castle, everywhere, everywhere, wherever he could see—one thousand silver eggs in all!

About the Author and Artist

Sylvia Cassedy writes: "Except for a short stay in Florence, my glimpses of the Tuscan landscape have been limited to those from railroad windows." In Pierino's story, though, imagination and a talent for language more than compensate for first-hand experience.

Mrs. Cassedy was born in Brooklyn and attended the Ethical Culture School there, "where everybody spent hours painting and sculpting and writing, long before creativity in the classroom became fashionable." In high school, she won several poetry awards, one of them national. In 1951, she received her B.A. from Brooklyn College and later studied in the Department of Writing Seminars at Johns Hopkins University.

Mrs. Cassedy and her husband, an associate professor at the Polytechnic Institute of Brooklyn, have three children, Ellen, Steven and Amy. They live in Great Neck, Long Island, New York.

Evaline Ness is the author and illustrator of a number of distinguished picture books for children, most recently *Tom Tit Tot* and *A Double Discovery*. Her illustrations for *All in the Morning Early* by Sorche Nic Leodhas (1964) and *A Pocketful of Cricket* by Rebecca Caudhill (1965) made those books runners-up for the Caldecott Award.

Miss Ness was born and grew up in Pontiac, Michigan. She has studied at the Chicago Art Institute, the Corcoran Gallery in Washington, D.C., and the *Accademia di Belle Arti* in Rome, and has had her paintings exhibited in two one-man shows. She now lives in New York City.